W9-BHZ-112

Watch Out, William!

Written by Nette Hilton
Illustrated by Beth Norling

An easy-to-read SOLO
for beginning readers

Scholastic Canada Ltd.
New York Toronto London Auckland Sydney
Mexico City New Delhi Hong Kong Buenos Aires

Scholastic Canada Ltd.
175 Hillmount Road, Markham, Ontario L6C 1Z7, Canada
Scholastic Inc.
555 Broadway, New York, NY 10012, USA
Scholastic Australia Pty Limited
PO Box 579, Gosford, NSW 2250, Australia
Scholastic New Zealand Limited
Private Bag 94407, Greenmount, Auckland, New Zealand
Scholastic Ltd.
Villiers House, Clarendon Avenue, Leamington Spa,
Warwickshire CV32 5PR, UK

Text copyright © Nette Hilton 1998
Illustrations copyright © Beth Norling 1998

Cover design by Lyn Mitchell

First published by Omnibus Books, part of the
SCHOLASTIC GROUP, Sydney, Australia.

National Library of Canada Cataloguing in Publication
Hilton, Nette
        Watch out, William! / Nette Hilton ; illustrated by Beth Norling.
ISBN 0-439-97440-2
I. Norling, Beth II. Title.
PZ7.H56775Wa 2003   j823'.914   C2002-905282-3

5 4 3 2 1   Printed and bound in Canada   3 4 5 6 / 0

For Melissa, a cyclist of style – N.H.

For Chris and Rosa – B.N.

Chapter 1

William had a fine bike. It was a
bright yellow BMX. The bell on the
handlebar gave a loud *ding! ding!*
and the tires were big and fat.

William couldn't ride his bike very well yet. He could walk with it, but it wobbled and bumped when he tried to get on.

His mum and dad gave him
a gold bicycle helmet with a big
flash of lightning down the side.
William wore it in the backyard
while he walked his bike.

Soon William could ride his bike
in the backyard and along the
side of the house.

When he felt a little braver, he rode very slowly all the way down to the corner store.

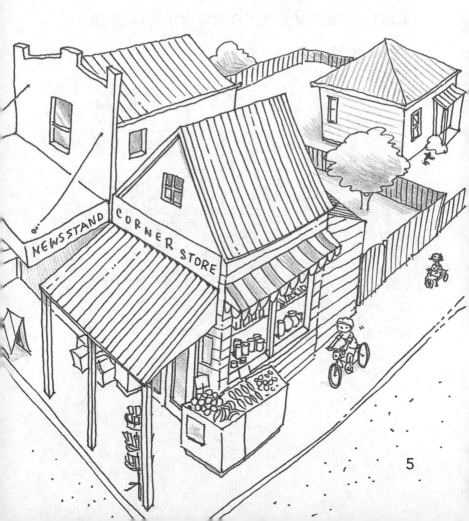

The shopkeeper, Mr. Purvis, was a friend of his.

"Watch out, William!" said Mr. Purvis as William wobbled past, nearly crashing into a pile of boxes.

"Uh-oh," said William.

Mr. Purvis smiled. "Don't worry," he said. "Before long you'll be riding like an Olympic champion."

Chapter 2

More than anything, William wanted to ride his bike to school. But it was a very long way, and he wasn't sure he was ready to ride that far.

What if there was a hole or a post in a place where it hadn't been before? His teacher, Ms. Samson, wouldn't like it if he arrived at school late, or muddy.

He decided that it would be much easier to *walk* the bike to school. And he did just that!

After school, William was worried all over again. Should he walk his bike, or ride it?

Ms. Samson made up his mind for him. "Hop in the bike line, William," she said. "And when I say Go, you pedal out the gate."

William hopped on his bike.

"Go!" yelled Ms. Samson.

Chapter 3

William took a deep breath. He pointed his bike to the left and pushed hard on the pedal. But he didn't see the big rock near his front wheel.

The bike didn't go left. It went right. Straight up the ramp of a cattle truck.

"*Moo!*" said Bessie the cow.

The truck driver, Mr. Swats, wheeled William down the ramp and gave him back his helmet.

"You'll be okay now," he said.
"Watch out for any more trucks!"

William held on tight to the handlebars and started to pedal. He was so busy watching out for trucks that he didn't notice where his bike was going.

It was taking him down a long
hill to the wrong side of an island.

Chapter 4

Ms. Peach was standing at the top of the hill with baby Imogen in her stroller. She was talking to Ms. Max and her dog Zeff.

Bounce, bounce, bounce went baby Imogen while she waited for her mother.

Rock, rock, rock went the stroller.

Twang! went the brake on the
stroller as it came loose.

Away went the stroller, and away went baby Imogen, faster and faster down the hill.

"My baby!" cried Ms. Peach. "Help! Somebody please save my baby!"

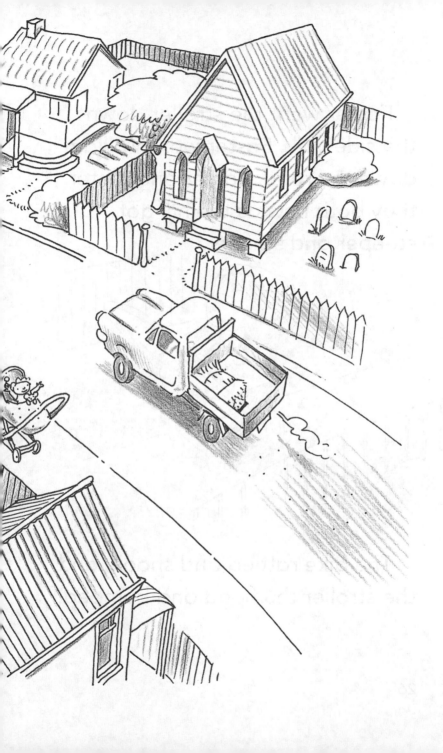

Faster went the stroller down the sidewalk. Faster went William down the road. Faster and faster they both flew as the hill got steeper and steeper.

The bike rattled and shook, and the stroller thumped and bumped.

William didn't fall off when Zeff tried to grab his wheel.

He didn't fall off when he bounced
over a huge hole in the road.

He didn't even fall off when his bike jumped up off the road and on to the sidewalk.

He hung on tight and just kept going.

Chapter 5

"Ga, ga, ga!" sang baby Imogen
when she saw William racing up
beside her.

By now William had stopped
watching out for trucks.

He could hardly see at all, because the wind had made his eyes fill with tears. But he knew that something white and bouncy was rushing along very close to him. He could hear it talking.

"Bubba, bubba, bubba!" it said. "Wheeeee!"

William tried hard to see what it was. He put out a foot to feel it. Then he pulled his foot back — or tried to.

"Oooooohhhhh!" said William.
He opened his eyes very wide.

His shoelace was stuck in the side of a big white baby stroller, and inside the stroller was baby Imogen Peach.

Chapter 6

"Help!" called Ms. Peach from a long way up the hill. "Somebody save my Imogen!"

William saw a Country Bakery truck in front of the corner store. A wide wooden ramp led up to its back door.

William looked hard at the ramp.
He knew exactly what to do.

"Hold on, Imogen!" he cried.

He leaned to one side, and he and the bike and Imogen and the stroller all flew across the sidewalk, over the curb, on to the road, up the ramp, and right into the back of the Country Bakery truck.

Chapter 7

"Uh-oh," said William as he wiped jellyroll off the seat of his pants.

"Uh-oh," he said again as he took three muffins away from

baby Imogen. "Uh-oh, uh-oh."
But nobody else seemed to mind.

"Hooray!" cried the truck driver.
"What a hero!"

"Bravo!" cried Ms. Peach, as
she gave William a big hug. "You
saved my baby!"

William looked at baby Imogen.
She had a round blob of whipped
cream on her nose. "I saved you,"
he said.

"Wheeeeee!" said baby Imogen.

William watched as Ms. Peach and baby Imogen and a lot of muffins set off up the hill. Baby Imogen waved to him all the way.

Chapter 8

Mr. Purvis held the bike ready for William to climb on.

"Well done, William," he said. "I knew you could do it! You rode your bike just like one of those Olympic champions!"

William was very happy. He
stretched his legs out and did four
little springy jumps, just like real
champions do.

"Thank you, Mr. Purvis," he said
as he climbed back on his bike.

He put his foot firmly on the pedal and smiled at the small crowd in front of the corner store.

As he pedalled away, he lifted his hand to wave.

Almost.

Nette Hilton

When I was young I wasn't very brave about riding my bike. I liked to ride close to fences so I could hold on if the wheels went one way and it looked like I was going another.

I can still remember the very first time I took one hand off the handlebar to wave to my friend. And I can still remember the very first time my bike took off and raced down the steepest hill in town. The wind rushed by so fast that all the world was a great big blur.

Writing about it was much more fun than doing it!

50

Beth Norling

I remember Dad teaching me how to ride a bike. I sat on the bike while he held on to the back of the seat. He ran, still holding on to the seat, and I pedalled. I was a bit like William and very nervous, so when I found out that I was riding along and Dad was no longer helping, I fell off!

Now I just get around on things with four wheels, but I can't wait till my baby is big enough to ride his tricycle.